W9-BLP-719

For Gilly,
who loves to dance
Love—N.D.

Papa Lucky's Shadow

story and pictures by

NIKI DALY

MARGARET K. MCELDERRY BOOKS
New York

Maxwell Macmillan International
New York   Oxford   Singapore   Sydney

*P*apa Lucky was a great mover. When he was young, he could dance the sequins off a champ.

Then, when he met Grandma, he put his dancing shoes away and took a steady job with Spare Hands Moving Company. But Ma says Papa Lucky never stopped dancing. Whenever music touched his ears, his feet would tap-tap and his fingers would snap-snap.

When Grandma died, Papa Lucky came to live with us. He got out his dancing shoes, had new steel taps fitted, and started talking about the old times again. Maybe he could earn some money dancing.

Ma said, "You're crazy. What will you look like dancing in the street?" Papa Lucky looked her straight in the eye and said, "Angel, I was hotfooting looong before you were born. Besides, these shoes are far from worn out."

Papa Lucky bought himself a real cool tape player.
Then he went around to the Pensioners' Club and taped
some music he and his buddy used to play in the old days.

Papa Lucky practiced every morning in the yard—the soft-shoe shuffle, the slide, and the Madison. I was put in charge of the music and got to know some of the Golden Oldies real well. Ma didn't like it at all and shook her head, but I thought Papa Lucky was great.

Sometimes we played "Me and My Shadow," and I would be Papa Lucky's shadow. Hanging out the washing, Ma would yell, "Don't put silly ideas into the girl's head, old man!"

Papa Lucky said I could be his "hat girl" and that we'd find a good place for our act in the city where money walks and money talks. So, early, before the shoppers hit the streets, Papa Lucky and I set up the tape player on the sidewalk in front of a fancy store.

"Sugar, you keep an eye on the hat and the coins that roll and I'll see to the rest," said Papa Lucky, tying his red shoelaces in a double knot.

Then Papa Lucky danced.

People stopped to look. Some threw coins. Some of the coins plinked into the hat, but others I had to chase. Some shoppers shook their heads, like Ma. Some smiled and moved in slow time to "Me and My Shadow" as Papa Lucky hotfooted over the city sidewalk.

Sometimes, Papa Lucky got a little dizzy.
Then we'd sit down and take five.

Later, on the bus going home, Papa Lucky counted the coins.
There were new ones and old ones and, among them all, a couple
of bottle tops.

Papa Lucky bought Ma a deluxe steam iron that had five different temperatures. "Now you can stop shaking your head like I'm a crazy man," he teased. Ma smiled and said, "As long as you don't put any ideas into the girl's head." Papa Lucky looked at me and winked.

The next day, before the Pensioners' Club party, Papa Lucky nailed a couple of bottle tops under my old school shoes. But we didn't tell Ma.

"Go, Sugar, go!" Papa Lucky laughed. His feet jived and bamboozled.
But I didn't miss a trick.

That's what it's like being Papa Lucky's shadow.

Margaret K. McElderry Books, Macmillan Publishing Company, 866 Third Avenue, New York, NY 10022

Macmillan Publishing Company is part of the Maxwell Communication Group of Companies.
First edition
Printed in Hong Kong by South China Printing Company (1988) Ltd.   10 9 8 7 6 5 4 3 2 1
The text of this book is set in Aster.   The illustrations are rendered in watercolor and pencil.

Library of Congress Cataloging-in-Publication Data
Daly, Niki.
Papa Lucky's shadow : story and pictures / by Niki Daly. — 1st ed.   p.   cm.
Summary: With his granddaughter's help, Papa Lucky takes his love of dancing onto the street and makes some extra money.
ISBN 0-689-50541-8
[1. Dancing—Fiction.   2. Street theater—Fiction.   3. Grandfathers—Fiction.]   I. Title.
PZ7.D1715Pap   1992   [E]—dc20   91-24283